A Birthday Wish

To _Julie_

From _JLS Board 94/95._

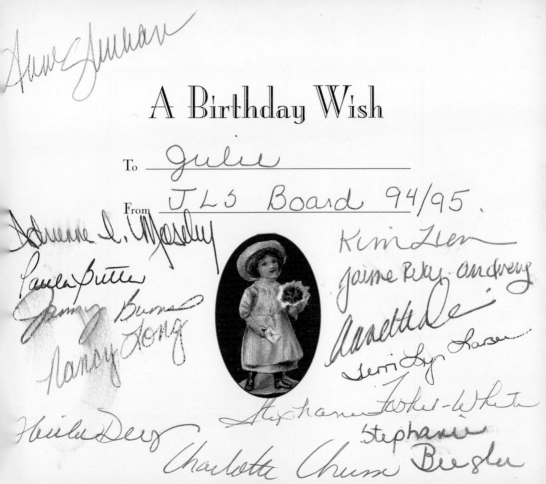

Anne Sullivan

Adrienne L. Moseley

Paula Pette

Jenny Burns

Nancy Long

Sheila Derry

Kim Zien

Jaime Riley Andrews

Annette Lei

Terri Lyn Larsen

Stephanie Fisher-White

Stephanie Biegler

Charlotte Chum

$\mathcal{B}$IRTH–1. The bearing of offspring.
Viewed as an act of the mother: a. Bringing
forth, giving birth. c. Viewed as a fact per-
taining to the offspring: The fact of being born,
nativity, beginning of individual existence, coming into the world.

Birth-carol, -pang, -peal, -song, -stead, -star

Birth-puffed—a. proud of one's descent

Birth-tide—birth time

—Sir James Murray
New English Dictionary
1888

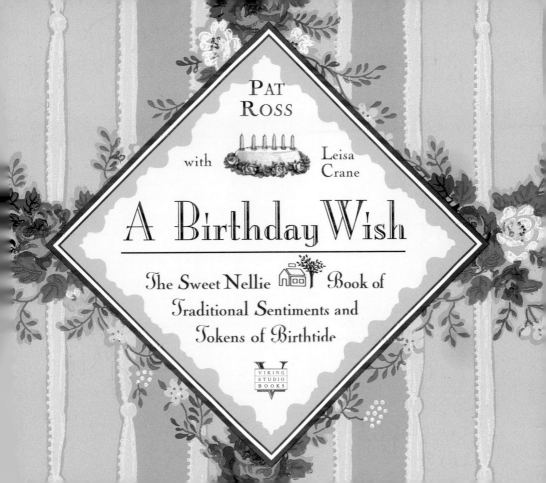

PAT ROSS

with Leisa Crane

A Birthday Wish

The Sweet Nellie Book of
Traditional Sentiments and
Tokens of Birthtide

VIKING
STUDIO
BOOKS

VIKING STUDIO BOOKS
Published by the Penguin Group
Penguin Books USA Inc., 375 Hudson Street, New York, New York 10014, U.S.A.
Penguin Books Ltd, 27 Wrights Lane, London W8 5TZ, England
Penguin Books Australia Ltd, Ringwood, Victoria, Australia
Penguin Books Canada Ltd, 10 Alcorn Avenue, Toronto, Ontario, Canada M4V 3B2
Penguin Books (N.Z.) Ltd, 182-190 Wairau Road, Auckland 10, New Zealand

Penguin Books Ltd, Registered Offices: Harmondsworth, Middlesex, England

First published in 1993 by Viking Penguin, a division of Penguin Books USA Inc.

1 3 5 7 9 10 8 6 4 2

Copyright © Pat Ross, 1993   All rights reserved

"The Birthday Child" by Rose Fyleman reprinted by
permission of The Society of Authors as the literary representative
of the Estate of Rose Fyleman

Library of Congress Cataloging-in-Publication Data
Ross, Pat
A brithday wish: the Sweet Nellie book of
traditional sentiments & tokens of birthtide / Pat Ross with Leisa Crane.
p. cm.
ISBN 0-670-84437-3
1. Birthdays. I. Crane, Leisa. II. Title
GT2430.R57 1993
394.2—dc20   92-24798

Printed in Japan
Set in Nicholas Cochin
Designed by Virginia Norey and Amy Hill

INTRODUCTION

We can count on being the center of attention one day of every year. Though our calendar is crammed with holidays and festive celebrations, our birthday is ours alone. Birthday customs reach back to ancient times, to Egypt and Mesopotamia, when only royal personages were entitled to celebrate the day with feasts, parades, circuses, even gladiatorial combat. Over time, the fashion for such grand events has waned in favor of more personal celebrations for everyone.

We may be unaware of distant folklore and legend, but it still plays a part in our special day. We can thank German tradition for the birthday cake, though our American version has abandoned the fruits, jams, and glazes in favor of layers deliciously frosted and prettily decorated. In Scandinavia, guests are still invited to share a pretzel-shaped cake and a pot of hot chocolate. History records that lighted candles started with the Greeks, who placed tapers on honey cakes, delivering them even to guests who were unable to attend. In folk belief, candles were endowed with special magic for granting wishes, which is why we always hope to extinguish the flames on the first try. It was believed that birthday greetings were most effective when spoken upon waking or at the stroke of midnight on the birthday eve, and more significant when written in longhand than printed. If you believe in the influence of the sun, moon, and the stars, as did our ancients, you may wish to listen to their prophecies and check your horoscope.

We are always pleased when someone remembers our birthday. And most of us have etched in our memories vivid recollections of those days, especially from childhood. We remember the cake along with the spilled milk, or the hesitant guest who needed coaxing to part with a gift clutched tight. I can still remember the blue velvet dress that my mother made for my fifth birthday party, perhaps because it felt so soft and looked so elegant, and was a token of love and labor (she had just taken up sewing).

It was a tradition in our family for the girls to be "started" on our silver pattern quite early so that we'd be ready to entertain for a crowd, I suppose, by the time we were "marriageable." So there in the center of my gifts was a fine wooden silverware box, large enough for many pieces but containing only one silver spoon. What a disappointment for a five-year-old! A nearly empty box and a spoon! Hardly a gift deserving a big thank you (as I'd been dutifully instructed) to the giver, a most proper aunt who anticipated my joyful appreciation. Seeking, perhaps, some childlike use for this gift, I hopped on top of it and, waving the shiny spoon, did a little tap dance in my new Mary Janes. My aunt was aghast, and my mother quickly ended my solo, but not before I had scratched the smooth surface of that fine box. Today, the small marks worn smooth by time, detectable only by me, remind me of the appropriateness of a gift, and a day many years ago recalled with clarity.

A Birthday Wish contains a sampling of birthday traditions as remembered by nineteenth- and early-twentieth-century writers, both well-known and anonymous. Their clear and vivid recollections tell of celebrations for young and old, party gifts and party favors; they impart advice from the zodiac, and supply philosophical *bon mots* that are ageless. Their thoughts have been gleaned from birthday albums, entertainment and etiquette guides of the day, vintage post cards and greeting cards, diaries, and poetry offerings. Even the most jaded palates will find something among these delectable souvenirs to make a loved one's birthday special.

Your Friend

Happy
Birthday to You

The shadow on the dial's face, that steals,
from day to day,
With slow, unseen, unceasing pace,
moments, and months, and years away;
This shadow, which, in every clime,
Since light and motion first began,
Hath held its course sublime.

—Frederick Saunders
Salad for the Solitary and the Social
1871

Do you count your birthdays thankfully?

—Horace
Epistles
19 B.C.

May the morning of thy birth break in gladness, and the day teem with light-hearted mirth that shall last always!

—J.S. Ogilvie
The Album Writer's Friend
1881

In consideration that Miss Annie H. Ide . . . was born out of all reason upon Christmas Day, and is therefore out of all justice denied the consolation and profit of a proper birthday; And considering that I . . . have attained an age when, O, we never mention it, and that I have no further use for a birthday of any description . . . Have transferred . . . to the said Annie H. Ide, all and whole my rights and privileges in the thirteenth day of November, formerly my birthday, now, hereby, and henceforth; the birthday of the said Annie H. Ide, to have, hold, exercise, and enjoy in the customary manner.

—Robert Louis Stevenson
1891

Hang all birthdays. I shall cut the memory of mine.

—John Ruskin
Diary
February 8, 1841

He that is not handsome at twenty,
Nor strong at thirty, nor rich at forty,
Nor wise at fifty, will never be
Handsome, strong, rich, or wise.

—George Herbert
Outlandish Proverbs
1640

Today's your natal day;
  Sweet flowers I bring:
Mother accept I pray
  My offering.

—Christina Rossetti
"To My Mother"
(Poem tucked into nosegay
for mother's birthday)
1841, age 11

$\mathcal{L}$ittle trouble and still less care,
With ever a faithful heart to share;
Birthdays many, and happy too,
This is the life I wish for you.

—J.S. Ogilvie
The Album Writer's Friend
1881

$\mathcal{I}$ do not wish you grandeur,
   I do not wish you wealth—
Only a contented mind,
   Peace, competence, and health;
Fond friends to love thee dearly,
   Honest ones to chide,
Faithful ones to leave to thee,
   Whatever may betide.

—Frances P. Sullivan
Standard Autograph Album Verses
1883

Star Bright

$\mathcal{B}$irthdays are intimately linked with the stars, since without the calendar, no one could tell when to celebrate his birthday.

—Ralph and Adelin Linton
The Lore of Birthdays
1952

$\mathcal{M}$y mother cried; but then there was a star danced, and under that I was born.

—William Shakespeare
Much Ado About Nothing
1599

Hood's Sarsaparilla Calendar 1892

Monday's child is fair of face,
Tuesday's child is full of grace,
Wednesday's child is full of woe,
Thursday's child has far to go,
Friday's child is loving and giving,
Saturday's child works hard
for its living,
But the child that's born on the
Sabbath day,
Is fair and wise and good and gay.

—Old Superstition

January

By her who in this month is born,
No gems save *Garnets* should be worn;
They will insure her constancy,
True friendship and fidelity.

February

The February born will find
Sincerity and peace of mind;
Freedom from passion and from care,
If they the *Pearl* will always wear.

March

Who in this world of ours their eyes
In March first open shall be wise;
In days of peril firm and brave,
And wear a *Bloodstone* to their grave.

April

She who from April dates her years,
Diamonds should wear, lest bitter tears
For vain repentance flow; this stone,
Emblem of innocence is known.

May

Who first beholds the light of day
In Spring's sweet flowery month of May
And wears an *Emerald* all her life,
Shall be a loved and happy wife.

June

Who comes with Summer to this earth
And owes to June her day of birth,
With ring of *Agate* on her hand,
Can health, wealth, and long life command.

July

The glowing *Ruby* should adorn
Those who in warm July are born,
Then will they be exempt and free
From love's doubt and anxiety.

August

Wear a *Sardonyx* or for thee
No conjugal felicity.
The August-born without this stone
'Tis said must live unloved and lone.

SEPTEMBER

A maiden born when Autumn leaves
Are rustling in September's breeze,
A *Sapphire* on her brow should bind,
'Twill cure diseases of the mind.

OCTOBER

October's child is born for woe,
And life's vicissitudes must know;
But lay an *Opal* on her breast,
And hope will lull those woes to rest.

NOVEMBER

Who first comes to this world below
With drear November's fog and snow
Should prize the *Topaz's* amber hue -
Emblem of friends and lovers true.

DECEMBER

If cold December gave you birth,
The month of snow and ice and mirth,
Place on your hand a *Turquoise* blue,
Success will bless whate'er you do.

—Author unknown
Notes and Queries
1889

$\mathscr{B}$IRTH FLOWERS

January - snowdrop
February - primrose
March - violet
April - daisy
May - hawthorn
June - wild rose
July - water lily
August - poppy
September - morning-glory
October - nasturtium
November - chrysanthemum
December - holly

—Traditional

The Children's Hour

I am old, so I can write a letter;
  My birthday lessons are done;
The lambs play always, they know no better;
  They are only one times one.

And show me your nest with the young ones in it;
  I will not steal them away;
I am old! you may trust me, linnet, linnet:
  I am seven times one today.

—Jean Ingelow
"Seven Times One"
1885

Everything's been different
  All the day long,
Lovely things have happened,
  Nothing has gone wrong.

Nobody has scolded me,
  Everyone has smiled.
Isn't it delicious
  To be a birthday child?

—Rose Fyleman
  "The Birthday Child"
  1928

𝒶 birthday cake must always have candles, and children dearly love the snapping cracker caps, and all the dainty favors which they take home. In fact the treasures that are taken home are half the party.

—Ellye Howell Glover
"Dame Curtsey's" Book of Etiquette
1930

At each child's place was a little cage, each one containing a bear, lion, tiger, or some other animal. The animals were of the papier-mâché variety and the cages were small gilded boxes with open fronts wrapped in gilt wire. There was also a package of chocolates wrapped in tinfoil and tied with bright ribbons.

BUTTON GAME

Tie pieces of cotton threads to pins bent up like fish hooks, having one for each child. Put a quantity of common shoe buttons in a tray and place it on a small table around which the children are seated with their fish hooks. The hooks are thrown out into the pile of buttons in an endeavor to catch a "fish." To the child who can catch the most button "fish" in five minutes should be given a prize. Of course, a child must not use his fingers to put the buttons on the hook.

—*How to Entertain at Home*
1927

C ry on your birthday, cry every day of the year.

—English nanny saying

I t is also a bad omen if the birthday cake
"falls," or if the weather is stormy.

—Ralph and Adelin Linton
The Lore of Birthdays
1952

KELLOGG'S EXTRACT,
GIVES A FINE FLAVOR TO CAKES AND CUSTARDS.

ALMOND.

$\mathcal{A}$t birthday parties the guests should be taught to offer congratulations by saying, "I wish you many happy returns of the day"; and it must be early taught children how to take leave by saying, "I have had a very happy time," or, "Thank you for the very pleasant party."

—Ellye Howell Glover
"Dame Curtsey's" Book of Etiquette
1930

Make A Wish

$\mathcal{T}$he birthday cake holds the place of honor on the table. Around the edge of it, in small tin holders, are candles—one for each year the child has thus far celebrated. $\mathcal{O}$ne candle is blown out by each little guest, and with it goes a secret wish of happiness for the boy or girl whose birthday it is.

—Lillian Eichler
Book of Etiquette
1922

The candles on your cake so bright
Are symbols of your radiant light,
And so all through the coming year
They'll light the path for you, my dear.

—Ellen Bellows Endicott
"Courage"
ca. 1939

$\mathcal{I}$t is their custom to honor their birthday above all other days; and on this day they furnish their table in a more plentiful manner than at other times.

—Herodotus
on the festivals of the Persians

My youngest son, Captain Irving Johnson, who sails his own ship *Yankee*, and cruises around the world, is fond of this cake as it keeps in any climate. I send him some wherever he is on his birthday, which is July 4, and for Christmas. He saved some to eat "rounding the horn" when he sailed on the *Peking*. It was also served when he married a Pitcairn Islander to a girl from Manga Reva on the deck of the *Yankee*.

—Imogene Wolcott
The Yankee Cookbook
1939

TOASTS FOR BIRTHDAYS

At your age . . . you should be careful.

May you grow younger each birthday.

A drink to the man who has gained a
year to-day, a man of worth.

May you enter heaven late.

—Ellye Howell Glover
*"Dame Curtsey's" Book of Novel Entertainment
for Every Day in the Year*
1907

There was music, there was dancing,
And the night was most entrancing,
As if fairyland and floral band were holding jubilee;
There was laughing, there was pouting,
There was singing, there was shouting,
And old and young together made a carnival of glee.

—Josephine Pollard
"The First Party"
ca. 1939

Birthday Souvenirs

Every gift ought to represent the giver in some way. Thus: the author should present a book; the sailor, shells and coral; the poet, his poems; the miner, a gem; the painter, his picture; and everybody else according to their taste.

—*Proper Etiquette*
or How to Behave In Society

VERSE TO SEND WITH A BIRTHDAY GIFT

As this auspicious day began the race
Of every virtue joined with every grace;
May you, who own them, welcome its return,
Till excellence like yours again is born.

—Ellye Howell Glover
"Dame Curtsey's" Book of
Novel Entertainments for
Every Day in the Year
1907

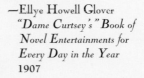

$\mathcal{A}$ plain dimity toilet cushion is one of the most useful and acceptable of gifts, and is easily and cheaply made.

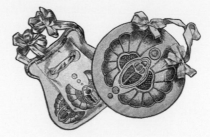

The pretty silk and satin scent-bags, which cost from fifty cents to a dollar at a perfumer's, may be made in a few minutes with a scrap of satin, a little piece of gold or silver cord to tie it up with, and sixpence worth of scented powder to enclose in the inside.

—Jennie June
Talks on Women's Topics
1864

Sometimes a friend of the mother will give the infant daughter a silver spoon, adding duplicates each year after on its birthday or at Christmas until they form a complete set.

—Lillian Eichler
Book of Etiquette
1922

A BIRTHDAY GREETING.

$\mathcal{L}$ ovingly take this birthday souvenir,
And for my sake esteem it dear!

—J. S. Ogilvie
The Album Writer's Friend
1881

" . . . There are three hundred and sixty-four days when you might get un-birthday presents. . . . And only *one* for birthday presents, you know. There's glory for you!" [said Humpty Dumpty to Alice].

❖

"Seven years and six months!" Humpty Dumpty repeated thoughtfully. "An uncomfortable sort of age. Now if you'd asked *my* advice, I'd have said 'Leave off at seven'—but it's too late now."

"I never ask advice about growing," Alice said indignantly.

"Too proud?" the other inquired.

Alice felt even more indignant at this suggestion. "I mean," she said, "that one can't help growing older."

–Lewis Carroll
Through the Looking-Glass
1871

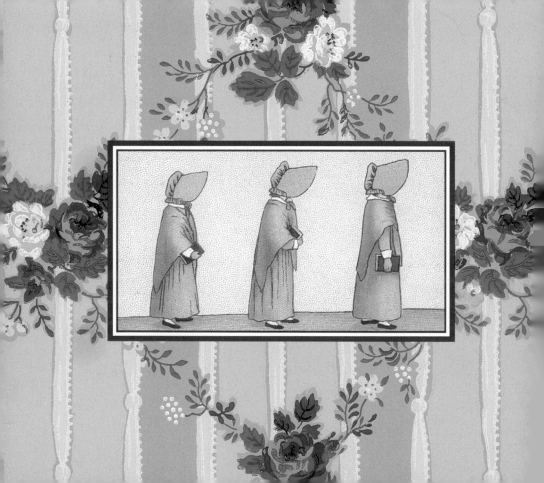

Much Wiser

$\mathcal{M}$ay beauty and truth,
　Keep you in youth;
Green tea and sage,
　Preserve your old age.

　　　　—J. S. Ogilvie
　　　　　The Album Writer's Friend
　　　　1881

$\mathcal{I}$f a woman is ever to be wise or sensible, the chances are that she will have become so somewhere between thirty and forty. Her natural good qualities will have developed; her evil ones will have either been partly subdued, or have overgrown her like rampant weeds. . . .

—A Woman's Thoughts About Women
1858

$\mathcal{M}$y birthday!—what a different sound
That word had in my youthful ears;
And how each time the day comes round,
Less and less white its mark appears.

—Thomas Moore
"My Birthday"
ca. 1845

At thirty a man suspects himself a fool;
Knows it at forty, and reforms his plan.

—Ellye Howell Glover
"Dame Curtsey's" Book of
Novel Entertainments for Every
Day in the Year
1907

Our birthdays are feathers
in the broad wing of time.

—Jean Paul Richter
Titan, XLVII
1803

People beyond threescore and ten often feel very young, for the soul does not age with the body, and while the house we live in falls apart, the soul is going on to immortal youth.

—Margaret E. Sangster
Good Manners for All Occasions
1904

For age is opportunity no less
Than youth itself,
  though in another dress,
And as the evening twilight
  fades away
The sky is filled with stars,
  invisible by day.

—Henry Wadsworth Longfellow
"Morituri Salutamus"
1875

I am not young enough to know everything.

—Sir James M. Barrie

$\mathcal{W}$e can't reach old age by another man's road.

—Mark Twain
"How to Reach Seventy"
1905

*I*t seems fitting that a book about traditions of the past should be decorated with period artwork. In keeping with the spirit of the book, the art in *A Birthday Wish* has been taken from personal collections of original nineteenth- and early twentieth-century party invitations, birthday cards, post cards, calendars, gift cards, trade cards, and other paper treasures of the time.

The endpapers and chapter openings contain patterns reproduced from some of our favorite vintage wallpapers.